The Brothers Grimm

Little Red Riding Hood

and other fairy tales

Miles
Kelly

First published in 2015 by Miles Kelly Publishing Ltd
Harding's Barn, Bardfield End Green, Thaxted, Essex, CM6 3PX, UK

2 4 6 8 10 9 7 5 3 1

Publishing Director Belinda Gallagher
Creative Director Jo Cowan
Editorial Director Rosie Neave
Designer Rob Hale
Production Manager Elizabeth Collins
Reprographics Stephan Davis, Jennifer Cozens, Thom Allaway

ISBN 978-1-78209-743-3

Printed in China

British Library Cataloguing-in-Publication Data
A catalogue record for this book is available from the British Library

ACKNOWLEDGEMENTS
The publishers would like to thank the following artists who have contributed to this book:

Front cover and all border illustrations: Louise Ellis (The Bright Agency)

Inside illustrations:
Little Red Riding Hood Ayesha Lopez (The Bright Agency)
The Golden Bird Martina Peluso (Advocate-art)
The Water of Life Atyeh Zeighami (Advocate-art)
The Rabbit's Bride Kristina Swarner (The Bright Agency)

Made with paper from a sustainable forest

www.mileskelly.net
info@mileskelly.net

Contents

Little Red Riding Hood

Once upon a time there was a little girl who was so kind and good that everyone loved her. Her grandmother gave her a special present – a hooded travelling cloak of red velvet. The little girl

thought it was so beautiful that from then on she never went out in anything else. So everyone called her 'Little Red Riding Hood'.

One day, the girl's mother said: "Little Red Riding Hood, your grandmother is ill. Will you visit her and take her this bottle of juice and her favourite cake? Hopefully they will do her good. Now, you know the way very well – make sure you don't leave the path, go straight there."

"Don't worry, mother," said Little Red Riding Hood, "I'll go straight there." She took the juice and cake and off she set through the woods to her grandmother's house.

She hadn't gone very far when a wolf trotted out of the trees up to her. Little Red

5

Riding Hood did not know that the wolf was sly and dangerous, so she wasn't at all afraid.

"Hello, Little Red Riding Hood," said the wolf, politely.

"Good day, Mr Wolf," said Little Red Riding Hood, and the wolf began to walk beside her.

"Where are you going?" he grinned.

"To my grandmother's," Little Red Riding Hood replied. "She's ill so I'm taking her some treats to help her feel better."

"And where does your grandmother live, Little Red Riding Hood?" asked the wolf.

"Just a few minutes further on," the girl replied. "Her cottage is the little one underneath the three large oak trees, you must have seen it."

Little Red Riding Hood never dreamed that the wolf was up to no good, but he was actually thinking:

7

'This little girl is so young and sweet, she would taste delicious! Maybe I can eat the grandma first, to stop my empty stomach rumbling, then this little girl second, as a sweet pudding...'

He quickly thought up a plan to slow Little Red Riding Hood down and be the first to reach the cottage. "How pretty the flowers are here," he remarked. "Why don't you pick some for your grandmother?"

"What a lovely idea," said Little Red Riding Hood, "thank you, Mr Wolf." And she skipped off into the trees to gather a pretty posy, while the wolf bounded off down the path, as fast as his legs could carry him.

Very soon he reached the grandmother's cottage and knocked gently at the door.

"Who's there?" came the sick old lady's weak, trembly voice.

The wolf tried to make his voice sound like Little Red Riding Hood's. "It's your granddaughter," he squeaked. "I've brought some treats for you. Open the door."

"How lovely – thank you!" called out the grandmother. "But I'm afraid I'm too weak to get up – just let yourself in."

The wolf licked his lips. He lifted the latch and pushed the door open. He sprang over to the grandmother's bed and swallowed her up with one *snap* of his jaws. Then he squeezed into her frilly nightdress and cap, drew the curtains together to darken the room, and lay down in her bed, pulling the covers over his chin.

Little Red Riding Hood arrived at the cottage to find the door wide open. 'How strange!' she thought. Nervously, she stepped inside to find the usually bright room all dim and gloomy. 'Very strange indeed,' she thought. There lay her grandmother with her nightcap pulled far down over her face and the covers drawn up over her chin, looking very odd.

"Oh, Grandmother," Little Red Riding

Hood said, "what big ears you have! I've never noticed before."

"All the better to hear you with, my dear," came the reply.

"Oh, Grandmother, what big eyes you have!" Little Red Riding Hood couldn't help but remark.

"All the better to see you with, my dear," came the reply.

"Oh, Grandmother, what large hands you have!" said Little Red Riding Hood, her eyes widening with surprise.

"All the better to hug you with, my dear," came the reply.

"Oh Grandmother! What a big mouth you have!" gasped Little Red Riding Hood.

"All the better to eat you with!" roared the wolf. And with that, he sprang out of bed and swallowed Little Red Riding Hood up.

The wolf now had such a full stomach that he began to feel very sleepy. Quite pleased with himself, he lay back down in the bed for a snooze.

But while he was snoring, a huntsman passed the cottage. The man thought it very unusual that the door was open wide and he looked in to see if everything was all right.

His eyes lit up when he saw the wolf in the bed. 'Ah, I have been trying to catch you for a long time!' he thought. He took out his hunting knife and – *slash, slash* – that was the end of the wicked creature… and out of the

slit in the wolf's tummy came Little Red Riding Hood and her grandmother! The wolf had swallowed them whole so, apart from being frightened, they were quite unharmed.

Then all three were delighted. The huntsman went home carrying the wolfskin. The grandmother admired the flowers, drank the juice and ate the cake and began to feel much better. And Little Red Riding Hood ran home safely to her mother and lived happily ever after.

The Golden Bird

There was once a king who had a beautiful garden with a tree which grew golden apples. Every day, it was the royal gardener's job to count the apples. But one morning, one was missing. It was the same

the next morning… and the next. The king was angry, so the gardener told his son to keep watch all night under the tree and see what was happening.

At midnight the young man heard a rustling noise. A golden bird came flying through the darkness. The gardener's son jumped up with his bow and arrow. As the golden bird snapped one of the apples into its beak, he let fly a shot. But the arrow only zipped through the bird's tail and a single feather fell to the ground.

Next morning, the gardener told the king what his son had seen and presented him with the golden feather. The king was stunned and called his wisest advisors to take

a look. Everyone agreed it was worth more than the king's whole treasure house. "I must have the whole bird!" ordered the king, greedily. So the gardener's son set out to find it.

He travelled in the direction the bird had flown until he came to the edge of a wood where a fox was sitting. "Sit upon my tail and you will travel faster," said the fox. The young man did so and away they sped over hills and fields.

Near a huge castle, the fox stopped.

"The soldiers are asleep," he told the gardener's son. "In a room you'll find the golden bird in a wooden cage. There will be an empty golden cage nearby, but don't try and swap the bird into that one or you'll wish you hadn't."

So the young man approached the castle, crept past the sleeping soldiers, and found the room with the golden bird. It was so beautiful that he couldn't bear to bring it away in such a dull old cage, and he swapped it into the golden cage after all. As he did so the bird let out an ear-splitting scream! The soldiers woke and took him prisoner and hauled him before the king.

"You will die for stealing my golden bird," announced the king, "unless you can bring me the golden horse. If you can do that, I will set you free – and I will let you take the golden bird too."

The gardener's son went back to the fox, ashamed. "Why didn't you do as I said?" scolded the fox. But he allowed the young man to climb onto his tail once more, and raced off with him to another castle. "Go into the stables and you'll find the golden horse," said the fox. "His groom will be asleep. But put the old leather saddle on the horse, not the golden one that is nearby."

So the young man crept into the stables, past the sleeping groom, and found the

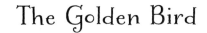

golden horse. He was so beautiful that he couldn't bear to put the old leather saddle on him, so instead he put the golden one on after all. As he did so the groom woke and shouted for the guards, who took the young man prisoner and hauled him before the king.

"You will die for stealing my golden horse," announced the king, "unless you can bring me the beautiful princess. If you can do that, I will set you free – and I will let you take the golden horse too."

So the gardener's son went back to the fox, even more ashamed. "Why didn't you do as I said?" scolded the fox, and raced off with him to a third castle. "At midnight, the princess will come out to bathe in the lake," the fox explained. "Go and give her a kiss and she'll come with you willingly – but make sure you don't let her go and say goodbye to her mother and father."

So the young man waited till midnight – and just as the fox had said, out came the princess to bathe in the lake. He went and gave her a kiss and she agreed to go away with him. However, she begged to go and say goodbye to her parents – and she was so beautiful that the gardener's son couldn't bear to refuse.

Of course the very moment the couple entered the castle, guards seized him for trying to steal the princess and hauled him before the king.

"You will die for stealing my daughter," announced the king, "unless in eight days you can dig away the hill that blocks the view from my window. If you can do that, I will set you free – and I will let you take my daughter too."

So the gardener's son hung his head in shame and started digging. After seven days the hill was hardly any smaller. Then the fox came to him and said, "Why didn't you do as I said? But lie down and go to sleep, I will work for you."

In the morning the young man awoke to find that the hill was entirely gone! The king could not believe his eyes, but he had to keep his promise and he allowed the gardener's son to leave with the beautiful princess.

"Now listen very carefully," the fox said to the gardener's son, "and I will tell you how you can keep all three: the princess, the horse and the bird."

This time, the gardener's son was determined not to make any mistakes. He did exactly as the fox said.

First, he took the beautiful princess to the king who wanted her. To his delight, the golden horse was brought out to him and he immediately leapt onto its back.

He reached down to the princess as though he wished to kiss her hand to say goodbye, but in one quick movement he seized her wrist, swung her up onto the

horse's back behind him,
spurred his steed on, and they were off,
as swift as the wind.

Then he took the golden horse to the king
who wanted him. To his delight, the golden
bird was brought out. "I must check that it
really is the right bird," the gardener's son

said – and as soon as the bird was in his hands he spurred the horse on once more, and they were off, as swift as the wind.

Finally, they took the golden bird to the king who wanted him. The king was so delighted that he not only let the gardener's son keep the golden horse and marry the beautiful princess, he also made him heir to his kingdom!

Then the fox came to him and said: "Now you must kill me. Trust me and do as I say." The young man did not want to do this at all, but he trusted the fox. He took a sword and did exactly as he had been told. At once there was a blinding flash and suddenly a handsome prince stood before him – it was

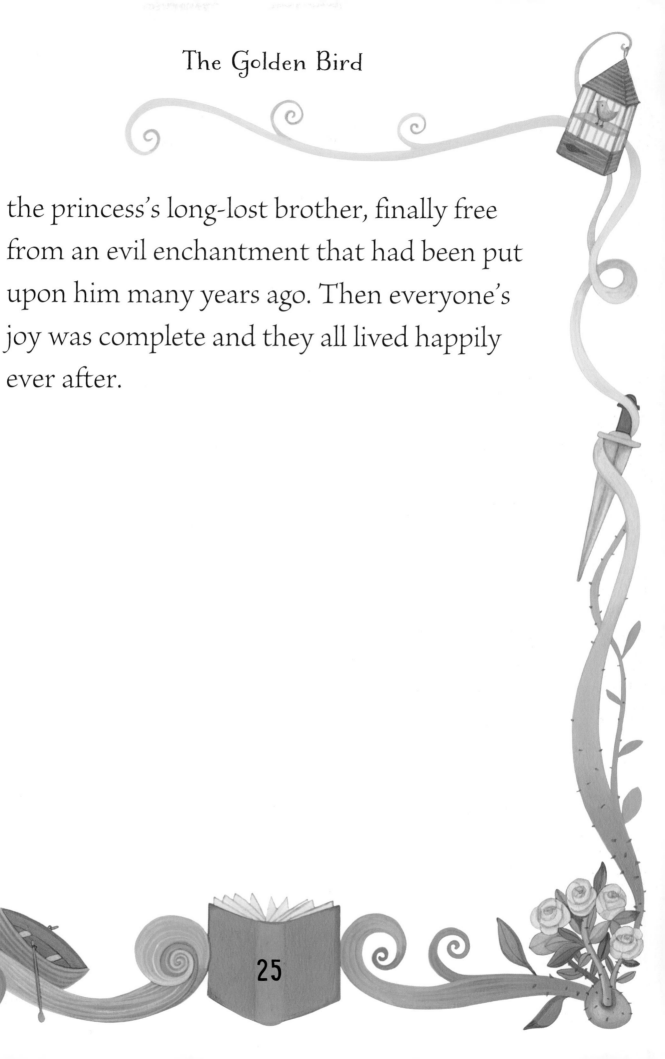

the princess's long-lost brother, finally free from an evil enchantment that had been put upon him many years ago. Then everyone's joy was complete and they all lived happily ever after.

The Water of Life

Long ago, there was a king in a far-off country who fell ill and was dying. His three sons were dreadfully upset. One day, as the young men walked together sadly in the palace gardens, a little old man appeared.

"I know something that would save your father," he whispered to them, "the Water of Life." And he vanished just as suddenly as he had arrived.

Later that day, the eldest son jumped on his horse and went galloping away from the castle. He was off to find the Water of Life – but not only because he did not want his father to die. He also thought that if he was the one to save the king, the king would give all his kingdom to him, and he would not have to share it with his brothers.

When he had travelled some way he rode into a gloomy, wooded valley. There, standing on a rock, was an ugly little dwarf.

"Where are you going?" cried the dwarf.

"What's it to you?" the prince shouted back.

The dwarf was so angry at the prince's rudeness that he muttered a magic spell. And as the prince rode on, the rocky hillsides on his right and left grew steeper and steeper. It became like riding through a narrow, rocky corridor. Then the path became completely blocked by boulders in front of him. He turned round to go back and saw that the path behind him had become completely blocked by boulders too. He was shut in on all sides! The prince jumped off his horse and discovered that he could not move a step – it was as if his feet were glued to the floor. He heard a loud laugh ringing through the air. And he had to stay there, spellbound.

Days passed and the eldest prince did not return to the palace, so the middle prince thought he would try to find the Water of Life. He too wanted to make his father better, but also thought he might win the kingdom.

The middle prince followed the same road as his elder brother. He also came across the dwarf – and was just as rude! The dwarf put the same spell on him and he also ended up spellbound in a rocky prison.

When the second prince had been gone a

long time, the youngest prince set out to search for the Water of Life. He wasn't bothered about being given the whole kingdom, he just wanted his father to be well.

He took the same road as his two brothers and met the dwarf at the same spot. But when the ugly little man called out, "Where are you going so fast?" the prince replied:

"I am searching for the Water of Life because my father is ill and going to die. But I have no idea where to find it. Please, can you help me?"

The dwarf was delighted that the prince had spoken so politely and he said: "You will find the Water of Life springing from a well in an enchanted castle. Here is an iron wand

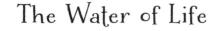

– when you reach the castle, hit the door three times with it and it will open. And here are two little loaves of bread – throw them to the lions waiting inside the door and they will not eat you up. Then hurry to fetch the Water of Life from the well. If the clock strikes twelve, the castle door will shut and you will be trapped there forever."

The prince thanked the dwarf many times and his new little friend showed him the road he should take to the enchanted castle.

After much hard riding, the prince arrived at the castle. Everything was as the dwarf had told him. At the third rap with the wand, the door flew open. When the lions were munching on the bread, he hurried on into

the depths of the castle, looking for the well.

At last, the prince finally found it, standing in one of the castle's beautiful courtyards. With trembling hands, the prince drew up a bucket of the precious Water of Life and poured it into a golden cup that stood at the edge of the well. Just then the clock began to strike...

One! Two! Three! The prince dashed back through the courtyards...

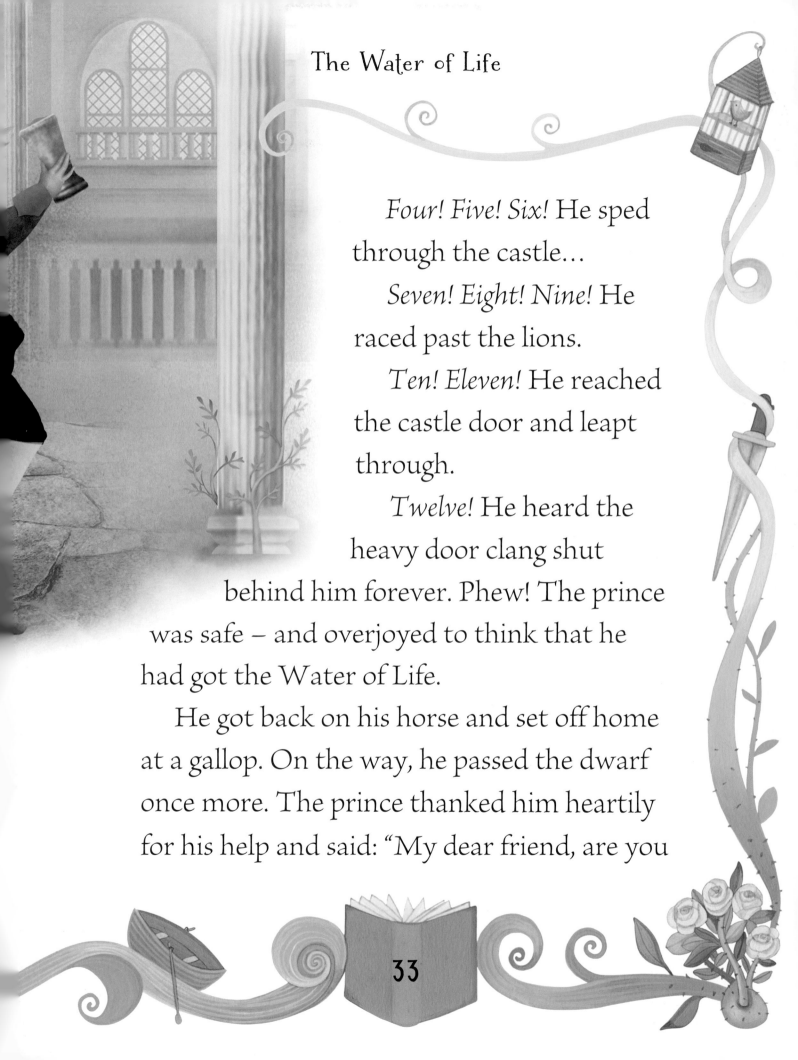

Four! Five! Six! He sped through the castle…

Seven! Eight! Nine! He raced past the lions.

Ten! Eleven! He reached the castle door and leapt through.

Twelve! He heard the heavy door clang shut behind him forever. Phew! The prince was safe – and overjoyed to think that he had got the Water of Life.

He got back on his horse and set off home at a gallop. On the way, he passed the dwarf once more. The prince thanked him heartily for his help and said: "My dear friend, are you able to tell me where my lost brothers are?"

The dwarf explained what had happened. Then he said, "They have learned their lesson – they will not be rude again," and he kindly returned the prince's brothers to him.

All three young men rode home together. The youngest son gave his father the Water of Life to drink and the king became well again. He arranged a splendid feast to celebrate his miraculous recovery – and of course the ugly little dwarf was the most important guest.

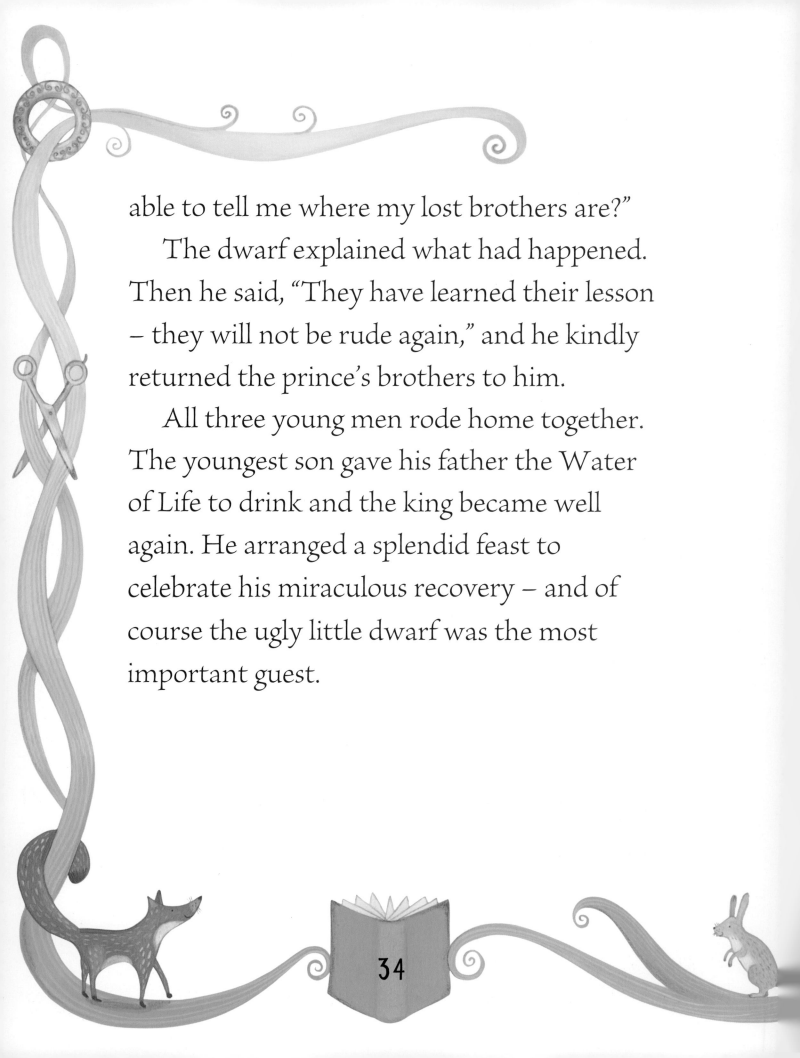

The Rabbit's Bride

There was once a woman who lived with her grown-up daughter in a little cottage. They had a vegetable patch where they grew prize cabbages. But one day a rabbit came and began to eat them all up.

The woman was annoyed and said to her daughter: "Get rid of that pesky rabbit!"

So the girl ran down the garden to the cabbage patch crying: "Shoo! Shoo! Don't you dare eat up all our cabbages, Mr Rabbit!"

To her surprise, the rabbit didn't scamper away. It turned and spoke to her. "My dear,"

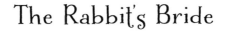

it said, twitching its fine long whiskers, "come and live with me in my burrow."

"Well I never!" said the girl, most put out. The rabbit shrugged and leapt away. The girl stomped back to the cottage.

The next day, the rabbit came back. And again the girl ran to the cabbage patch crying: "Shoo! Shoo! Don't you dare eat up all our cabbages, Mr Rabbit!"

"Well, have you thought about what I said?" the rabbit said, wiggling his soft tail at her cheekily. "Will you come and live with me in my burrow?"

"Certainly not!" said the girl, in a huff. The rabbit just shrugged and leapt away, and the girl strode back angrily to the cottage.

The following day, there was the rabbit again. And for the third time, the girl ran to the cabbage patch crying: "Shoo! Shoo! Don't you dare eat up all our cabbages, Mr Rabbit!"

"So," said the rabbit, winking at her, "are you going to come and live with me in my burrow or not?"

Suddenly, the girl had an idea. "All right," she said.

The rabbit beamed. "Hop on to my tail and I'll take you there," he said. So the girl did so and away they went.

When they reached the burrow, the rabbit let the girl down from his tail and said: "Now, you get to work and prepare a feast. I am going to tell all my family and friends the

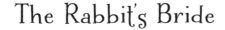

good news, and invite them to the wedding."

So the girl began to cook and the rabbit scuttled away and left her on her own.

As soon as the rabbit had gone, the girl took some straw and tied it with twine to make a figure about the same size and shape as herself. Then she dressed it in her own clothes. Next, she painted a face on it. Finally, she sat the figure in front of the oven so that it looked like it was keeping an eye on the cooking, and then she ran all the way home to her mother.

After a while the rabbit returned to the burrow. "Hello my dear," he said, "how are you getting on with everything?" and he went over and put his paw around the straw figure, which he thought was the girl. But as he touched it the figure's head fell off and rolled away across the kitchen floor!

"Oh my goodness!" gasped the rabbit, quite horrified. "I've killed her!"

And he scampered away, as fast as his legs could leap.

I have heard tell that the rabbit settled in a new home far away and found a lovely lady rabbit who was very happy to be his wife – but that may only be gossip. One thing's for sure: the woman, the girl and their cabbages were never bothered by rabbits again.